Introducing Hairietta Hairison The One, The Only Me

A Hair-oic Tale

To Jack, this one's for you and the trophy
we won at the daddy daughter date
for the Dad with the least amount of hair.
I was so proud.

-J.Z.

To my Mom whose faith never failed
in spite of it all.

-M.Z.

To my children who all
started out bald.

-S.Z.

www.jozybooks.com
ISBN 978-0-615-38305-7
Also available by Jo Zumbrunnen:
The Ugly Girl

Introducing
Hairietta Hairison
The One, The Only Me

Written by Jo Zumbrunnen
Illustrated by Shawn Zumbrunnen
Graphic Design by Michelle Zumbrunnen

For

My Granddaughters: Brenna, MacKenna, Sofi, Sienna, Josie, Sami and Hannah.
"Enjoy a part of each and every day, come what may."

-Grandma Jo

Testimonials

"A real page turner with a hair-raising ending."
— Abbey A. Roads

(**Teenager**, high school student, part-time ski instructor, part-time nanny and aspiring actress.)

"A hair-larious tale. It kept me in stitches."
—Mrs. Sofia Hannah Bills

(Retired first grade **Teacher**. Hobbies: ceramics, water aerobics and Red Cross volunteer. ... She hands out the cookies.)

Testimonials

"A story with a moral. Hair today, gone tomorrow."
- Molly Morison

(Her triplets Brenna, MacKenna and Sienna could not put it down. Stay at home **Mother** and co-author of *101 Ways to Cook With Spam*.)

"A quick read with a hairy plot."
- Mary Josephine Samantha Ann Harper

(Southern belle, beauty queen contestant and runner-up in four out of seven counties. Owner of Mary Jo's **Beauty Guru**, located on Main Street U.S.A.)

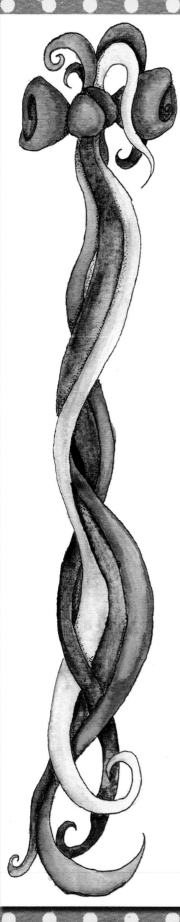

Hairietta Hairison,
born five weeks early,
a dimple on each cheek,
a voice that could shriek.

Skin so fair
and not any hair.
She did not care!

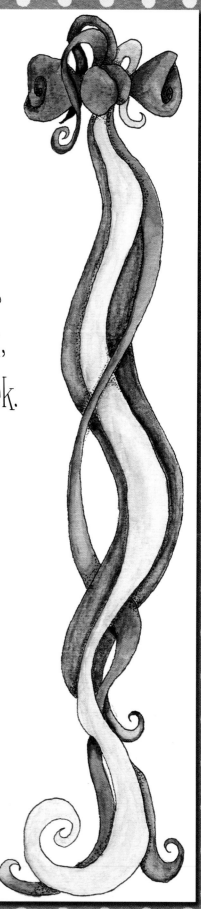

Hairold and Henrietta
Hairison

are happy to announce the birth
of their new baby girl
Hairietta;
born July 19th,
4 lbs, 10 oz,
23" long.

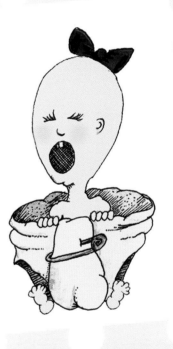

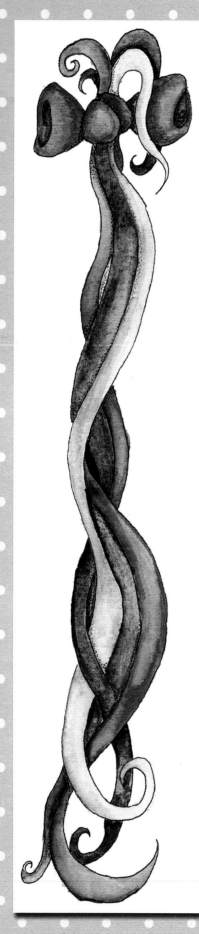

As time went on
curls appeared,
her head no longer
shiny and bare.

The color of chestnuts
in the autumn sun.

STUNNING
BEAUTEOUS
RADIANT
GORGEOUS
FLOWING
LOVELY
Hair.

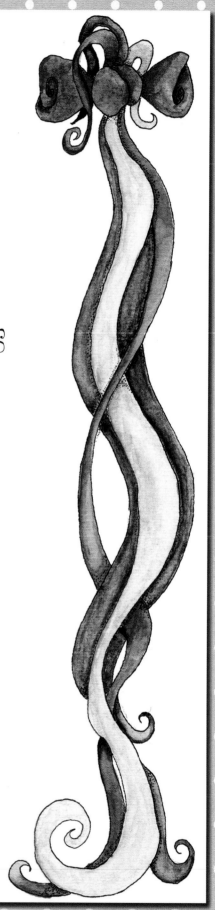

She did not care.

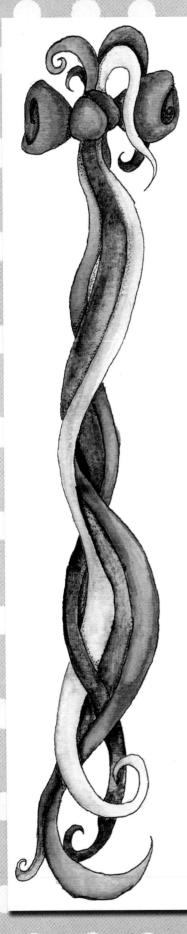
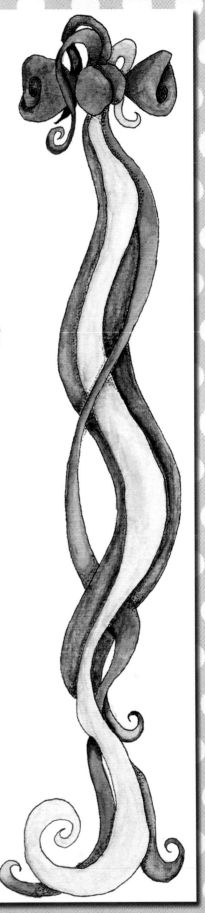

Hairietta was
learning to
hop, skip and jump;
run races with cousins
and play at the park.

She had a fish named
Dorothy and dreams
of a puppy.
she was barely
afraid of the dark.

Hop Skip Jump

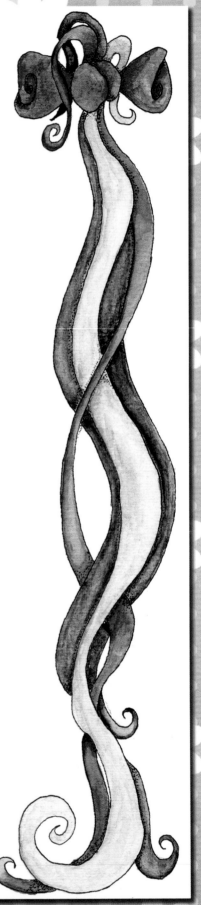

Hairietta was happy,
yes happy indeed.
She stood up tall
and shouted with glee.

"I'm Hairietta Hairison
the one,
the only
me!"

Super
Girl

Her hair absolutely fabulous
down her back in a braid.
Reading, painting, soccer and a little ballet.

Now if you think
this is where the
story will end,
just the opposite is true,
for this is where it began.

On the first day of Hairietta's
life in junior high,
her hopes and dreams
as high as the sky.

Track, basketball, dance
and theater too.
So many things
for a girl to do.

When she looked in the mirror
ready to shout for glee,
most of her hair was gone,
there were only three.

Three strands of hair
staring back at her,
when a great idea
simply occurred.

3 Hairs?!

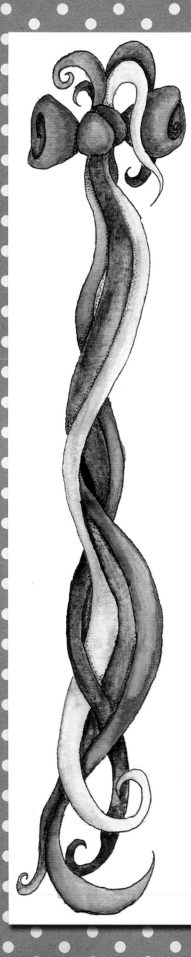
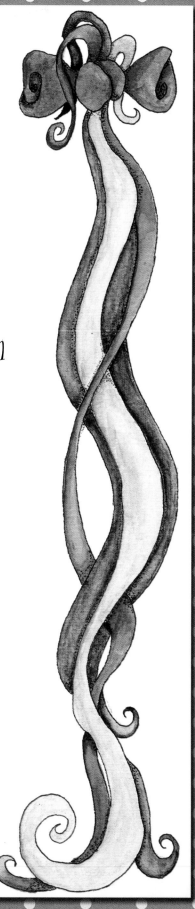

"Today I will braid it!"
she shouted with glee.
"I'm Hairietta Hairison
the one, the only me!"

Then off she went
to sign up for track,
grabbing an apple
and her backpack.

The next day, not three,
only two she could see.
"Piggy tails!"
she shouted with glee.
"I'm Hairietta Hairison
the one, the only
me!"

Today was dance class.
She grabbed her
ballet shoes.
So many things
for a girl to choose.

On the third day of school
and ready for fun,
she looked in the mirror
and saw only one!

"Today it's a pony!"
she shouted with glee.
"I'm Hairietta Hairison
the one, the only me!"

Onward to tryouts
for the school play.
So much to do,
so little time in a day.

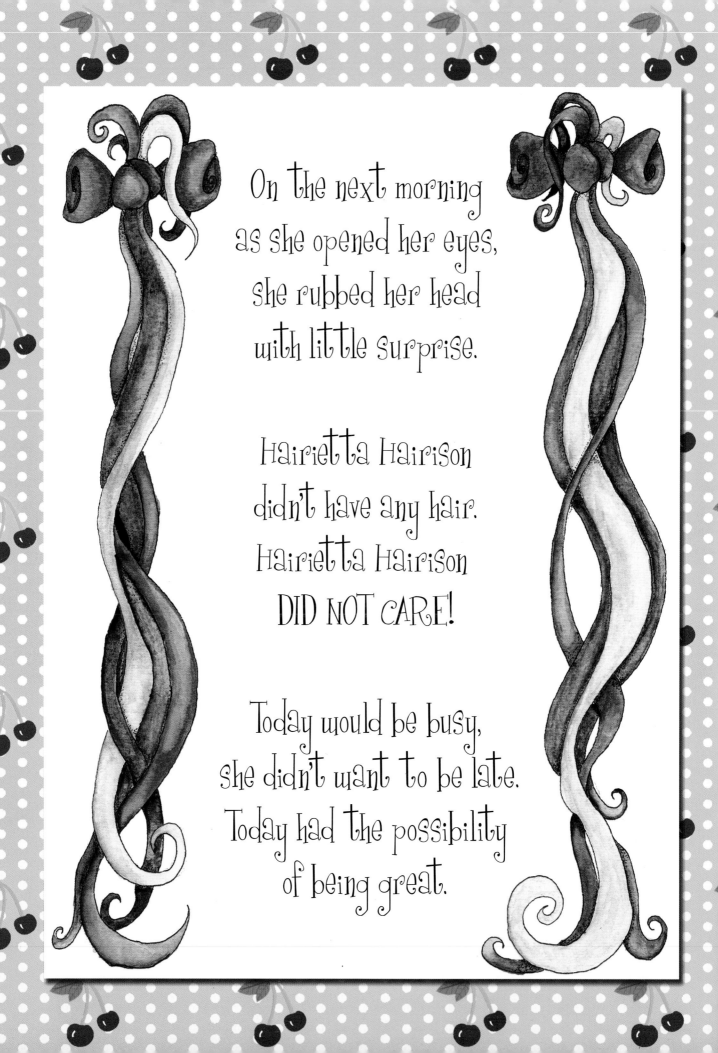

On the next morning
as she opened her eyes,
she rubbed her head
with little surprise.

Hairietta Hairison
didn't have any hair.
Hairietta Hairison
DID NOT CARE!

Today would be busy,
she didn't want to be late.
Today had the possibility
of being great.

Doesn't matter, a wee lass or a toddler of two.

A Teenager

A Teacher

A Mother

A Beauty Guru

Seven or forty,
one hundred and one,
you're the girl in charge,
now go have fun!

Oh remember, remember
long hair, short, curly,
thick or thin.
Look in the mirror
and put on your grin.

Then throw your head back
and shout for glee...

I'm

_____

(Your Name)

the one,
the only
ME!

The End